MW00884954

COLOR AND CUT CHRISTMAS FUN

Easy Designs for Kids to Color and Practice Scissor Skills

IVY MAPLEWOOD

Copyright © 2024 Ivy Maplewood
All rights reserved

ISBN-13: 979-8341342163

No part of this book may be reproduced in any form or by any electronic or mechanical means including information storage and retrieval systems, without permission in writing from the author. The only exception is by a reviewer, who may quote short excerpts in a review.

THIS COLORING BOOK BELONGS TO:

_____

*Each page is single-sided to minimize bleed-through. To further prevent any ink bleed from markers or pens, it's recommended to place an extra sheet of paper or cardstock behind the page you're coloring.

Made in the USA
Las Vegas, NV
30 November 2024

13035501R00046